THE DIARY FROM THE SHIRT POCKET OF AMERICA

Kelly Fernandez

ISBN-13: 9798667905233
ISBN-10: 1477123456

Cover design and Illustrations by: Kelly Fernandez
Library of Congress Control Number: 2018675309
Printed in the United States of America

This book is dedicated to all the American small towns that know everyone else's business, to every bar and cafe that has served as a place for those to go who have nowhere else to go, and to every teacher who encourages children to explore their creative talents.

INTRODUCTION

I've been trying to figure out how to tell this story. I've been trying to decide the best way to connect with readers and trigger nostalgia of our lost and twisted memories. I aim to communicate my thought space that lives between discomfort and reflection. I want to share strange experiences with characters that live within our reality and mostly characters that live within our minds.

CONTENTS

PART ONE: DEAR DIARY

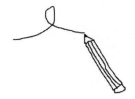

THAT FEELING IN YOUR STOMACH

Laying in my parent's big bed during the day,
I feel that kind of sudden pressure,
A feeling in my stomach.
Oh I know it is gonna hurt,
It makes me panic a little.
I wish it would just go away,
I want it to go away.
I don't want to get up,
I don't want to see mom,
I just want to lay here,
I just want it to go away.

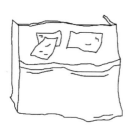

But now I know better,
Because I am getting older.

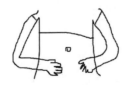

And I have to go poop.

I roll out of the bed,
Walking to my room,
I better be quick
I know it is coming soon.
I have to talk to someone,
Talk to get through it.
Walk up to my play kitchen,
That is where my microwave is.
I hold the countertop,
Face the microwave door,
I begin pushing.
Me and the microwave,

We both whisper,
"It's okay."
And I think, push.
Push. Squeeze. Push. Squish.
"It's okay," it whispers.
And I think, I'm doing it.
Push. Squeeze. Push. Squish.
"It's okay," it whispers.
And I think, I'm doing great.
Push. Squeeze. Push. Squish.
"It's okay," it says.
And I think, keep going.
Push. Squeeze. Push. Squish.
I push,
Until it is all over.
I don't cry,
It just hurts a lot.
"Thank you," I say a few times to the microwave.
I do not poop without it.

LA MENTIRA

When I was this young,
I lied a lot and felt very right to do so.
I felt like I needed to lie and I'm not sure why.
If you were a nice babysitter and gave me a hug,
I would tell my mom that I saw you pee in the bath-
tub.
If you were a responsible babysitter and fixed

mom's table legs,
I would tell my dad that your boyfriend came over
and cooked you scrambled eggs.
If you are nice enough to watch me at your own
house,
I would tell someone that I saw up your blouse.

VIOLENCE

I play Joseph in the play because I want to hold the
cane,
I use it to stab a boy twice in the foot and he screams
in pain.
He sits in the seat I want,
So I scratch him in the neck so he knows his place.
Teacher says please don't run with scissors.
I say I wasn't going to cut anyone's face.
"Clean up, clean up, everybody do your share…"
Sing the song,
Order others around 'cause I don't share or care.

"Stand up.
What do you have to say to your classmates?"
I am sorry.
For myself.
"Sit down."

THE TRUTH

"Oh, I wish your dad would come home."

NEIGHBORHOOD RULE BOOK

- No shoes allowed
- Know each family by their smell
- Boys play the dog in Barbies
- No kids in the deep end
- My house for junk food
- Hers for dress up
- Babysitters must be best friends
- The secret place must stay a secret
- Walk each other's dogs
- Stay out of dad's office
- Lights out is for teenagers

FAMILY RESTAURANTS

Pink tank top and pink cowgirl hat from Grandma's,
Sunroof open,
Lots of people walking around town.
Dad parks, and we are going to the bar.
Everyone's there.
The best pizza, the best games.
Outside, that cute boy from my school bus.
He's with his parents.

I want him to see me.
I hop up on the window ledge,
Lean back on my arms,
Hat tipped,
Can't see my eyes.
He frowns,
Squints,
Waves,
Turns away.

WARNINGS FROM YOUR TEACHER

"Will you be my friend?"
"Please leave me alone."
"Why? I just want to be your friend."
"I don't want to be your friend."
"Why?"
"I want you to leave me alone!"
"If you won't be my friend, I'm gonna tell on you!"
"Don't."
"I will."
"Please don't, I just don't want to be your friend!"

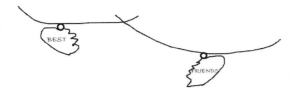

AT THE CORNER
OF MY EYE

She teaches me how to climb the tree by climbing
ahead of me,
Always pointing to where I could put my hands and
feet.
That's the way I go,
Unless someone was willing to show me another
way.
Some kids always climb way ahead of us,
And sometimes try to make us go away.
"I'm gonna try something different today."
"What are you doing?"
"I don't know,
I want to climb away from the trunk."
She teaches me how to know if a branch was dead,

She teaches me that hollow means empty.
"Can I follow you?"
"I'm just trying stuff right now,
I don't really know what I'm doing."
So I follow,
I use my lessons.

Just be careful,
Keep a close eye,
Hug the tree,
Grab the branch,
Move your foot.
And then I'm here.

I have a whole new view,
I can see the treehouse.
I have never been here before.
I did it.
But in the corner of my eye I see something,
I turn to see what it is,
A dirty shoelace tied to a dead branch.
I fall backwards,
Screaming, but not for long,
Before I hit the ground.

AN ETERNAL UNSPOKEN THOUGHT

I wanna go home.

WOUNDS

Mom wrapped my hand in white gauze,
So no one could see the rock stuck inside.
Mom dressed me in a long-sleeved shirt,
So no one could see the scab on my elbow.
I couldn't wait to show everyone,
I couldn't wait to show the boys.
On the bus, rolling up my sleeve,
"That is disgusting."
"What in the world."
"Get it out of here."
I feel proud.
I feel strong.
"How did it happen?"
"It looks like it hurts."
"Did you bleed?"
"Was it fun?"
"WHISPER," the bus driver shouts.

SCHOOL BUSES IN LINE

First is the worst,
Wave at the kids in front,

Second is the best,
Wave at the kids behind,
And third is the one with the Treasure Chest.
Kiss the twins up front,
Jump in the aisle,
Listen to cuss words,
Learn new bands,
Rumors about Santa,
Then you hold hands,
Three to a seat,
Defend your friend,
Ask why he is crying,
Hide under your seat,
The driver is coming,
Big boy is getting beat,
"Stay in your assigned seats."
Then I can only see the backs of heads,
I wave through the mirror,
They give me the finger instead.

WHEN MOM
DIDN'T
WORK

"I don't feel good.
I have a stomachache."
Mom picks me up like she should,
Piece of cake.

WARNINGS FROM YOUR TEACHER PART II

Tornado Drill.
"Sit in a line,
On the floor,
Against the wall…"
Hand raised.
"Yes?"
"How will he get there?
With his broken foot,
In a wheelchair?"
"Don't worry,

Just do as you should."

SECOND CRUSH

He has boogers running down both sides of his nose
holes.
He is cute and also has some really big moles.
I lean forward and whisper,
"I fell out of a tree and there is a rock stuck in my
hand,
Do you wanna see?"
He shrugs.
I am excited because he is all about me.

NOTICING ELEMENTS

It is a golden colored day,
My favorite color of day.
It takes a while to figure out how,
One school day I kind of figure it out.
Thunderstorm warning,
Everyone is loud.
I lie about a tree hitting my house,
The power goes out.
Out the window,
No darkness,
No clouds,
It was a type of light out,
"I love that color!"
I shout to nobody at all.

NOTICING PROBLEMS

Riding down the long green hills,
Getting close to the fence and field with horses.
Stop sign.
I see a flipped over truck,
On the other side of the ditch.
My seat buddy glances,
Just to look over.
I lean forward
Look closer.
No people.
Just this flipped over truck.
Bus keeps going.
Whispers behind me,
"Did you see that truck?"
"Yeah, it was a flipped over truck,"
Her voice was so calm,
It surprises me,

So much,
I think it is so funny,
I can't help myself,
It just happens,
I start laughing,
Loudly,
With no control
"WHO IS IT?"
The bus driver screams.
Fingers all pointing at me.

BOOK FAIR

"You can see what I circled, but don't circle the same books as me."
"Why not?"
"Because I want those books and I don't want them to run out."
"They have a bunch of them, we can get the same books!
Don't be mean."
"Just in case, I don't want them to run out so maybe you guys can look for your own books."
"We will do what we want."
I circle
Awful Ogre's Awful Day
Olivia Saves the Circus,
Sun Bread--
But then I see the videos.
I check

'Alice and Wonderland'
It is already gone.
I look for the boys,
No way they grabbed it.
I was ahead of them,
Someone else must have it.
"No," I whisper to myself,
So upset.
I go home
With 'Quest For Camelot'.

NOTICING ELEMENTS
PART II

It is close to when it gets dark,
The sun is at eye level with me through the car win-
dow.
What I don't understand
Is how the sun is always everywhere I am.
Mom is driving fast,
Faster than people run,
And there is the sun,
Going the same fast as us.
Why?
Why me?
Why will it follow me?
Not even follow,
It will always be there,
So I can see it,

As long as there are no clouds.
What about others?
Why is it always where I am,
And not where other people are?
How can it go as fast as we go?
I love it,
But I don't get it.

CAUGHT

"Their mom said she has heard an awful lot about you.
I asked what all she had heard about you,
Hoping she would say what a nice girl you are.
She said what she heard about you was all about kissing.
Lots of kissing."
The feeling in my stomach,
They told on me.
They told their mom,
Their mom told my mom,
My mom knows I've been kissing,
I start crying.
"You know I'm not mad, right?
What's going on?

Why are you kissing?"
No,
I didn't do anything wrong,
They didn't do anything wrong.
"Are you lying to me?"
I lie,
No,
I don't want to talk about it.
"You are making this worse.
Are you saying they are lying?"
No,
I didn't do anything wrong,
They didn't do anything wrong.
"Someone isn't telling the truth.
Should I call their mom?"
No.
"Should I talk to them?"
No.
"Relax,
I don't know why you are so upset.
You know their mom isn't mad, right?
They aren't upset either.
They just said you attack them and kiss them."
I know it is good they told the truth
I don't like that they told the truth.
"You're not in trouble,
What's going on?
Why are you kissing?
You need to relax,
Talk to me like a big kid.
Especially if you kiss like a big kid.

Have you kissed anyone else?
Are you okay?
I'll leave you alone now.
May I tell your dad?
I won't."

VIOLENCE PART II

"Can I see that?"
He tosses it over.
"Sweet," I smile.
I run downstairs,
Turn the corner,
Run for dad's secret office.
Run past the foosball table,
Run past the pool table,
Past the dart board,
Past the movie posters,
Past the drum set,
Up to his door.
I stand in the doorway,
Out of breath,
So excited.
Dad listens to someone talk on a speaker,
Leans back in his chair,
Looks over at me,
I walk up to him,
Put the gun to the side of his head,

Put my finger on the trigger -
"Whoa,
What the hell is this?"
Dad takes the gun from my hand,
Starting to look all serious,
I don't know why.
He looks at the gun,
Turns it over,
Looks at me with those eyes,
Wild eyes.
"Where did you get this?"
I tell him,
"He left it here."
Dad looks at the gun,
Dad looks at me.
"Do you know how serious this is?"
He looks at me more,
"Do you think this is a toy?"
"It is a toy, dad."
"No,"
Dad shakes his head,
Lays his cigarette in an ashtray.
"Guns are never toys."
He holds the gun in both his hands,
Pulls the trigger.
"Oh my God,
This part moves back and forth when you shoot it."
He looks at me,
"You know if you would have pulled that trigger,
I would have felt that?"
I look back at him,

I shake my head.
I didn't do anything wrong.
"Come here,
I want to show you something."
Dad puts his cigarette out,
Turns off the stereo,
Points to the door.
"Let's go,
Upstairs."
A long walk to mom and dad's room.
Hot feeling in my chest,
For some reason,
I'm in trouble.
Dad leads me to his closet.
"Have a seat,"
He points to the ground.
"What I am about to show you,"
He puts his hands on my shoulders,
"You cannot tell anyone about, okay?
This is our secret.
It is very, very important."
"Okay."
He lets go,
Pulls out the safe.
"Has your mother ever shown this to you before?"
"I've seen it before, when I've been in here."
"So have you ever seen what is inside?"
He turns the dial,
Opens the door,
I sit up to look inside,
"No,"

He pushes me back.
"You don't need to see everything that is in here,
Just sit down."
As I sit down,
He pulls out a gun.
He holds the side of the gun in front of my face.
It looks like the toy gun,
Except it is black.
"Do you know what this is?"
"It is a gun."
He holds the gun the way you do when you shoot it,
Toward his suits.
"This is not just a gun,
This is a pistol.
Not a toy,
This is real.
I have this around to keep you and your mother safe.
In case God forbid a bad guy would break in.
I'm going to tell you a story, okay?"
"Okay."
"When I was a little boy,
But much older than you,
I was ten years old.
Do you know where I grew up?"
"Bronx."
When dad was in a rush,
He would say,
"Everybody get out of my way,
I'm from the Bronx."
"That's right,
I'm from the Bronx.

Do you know anything about where I grew up in the
Bronx?"
"No."
He chuckles,
"Where I grew up,
Is not like where you are growing up.
Where I grew up,
It was dangerous.
Lots of ways to get in trouble,
Lots of bad guys,
Where I grew up,
You grow up much faster than where you are grow-
ing up."
Dad sits beside me,
Gun in his lap.
"One time,
I was hanging with a couple of my friends,
And my cousin on our street.
I'd been hanging with these guys for a long time,
Since I was your age.
I trusted them,
They trusted me.
On this day,
Our lifelong friend came with his gun,
Just like this one,
A pistol.
Not a toy.
He found it in his coffee table drawer.
We all passed it around,
We held it.
I remember when it was passed to me,

I held it,
It was so heavy."
Dad places the pistol on top of the safe,
Picks up the other gun,
"This toy you have here?"
He pulls the trigger over and over,
"This toy, it is light,
Hold it again."
He tosses it to me,
I hold it,
I know it's not heavy,
It is not hard to hold.
"How does it feel?"
"Light."
"And that is what pisses me off so much about you coming up to me in my office and pulling that trigger on the side of my head. Because it was so easy for you to hold that plastic piece of shit up and think that it is a joke."
Dark circles under dad's dark eyes,
Just like mine.
But he can look scary.
He takes the plastic from my hands,
Grabs the pistol,
"Now hold this with both hands."
I cup my hands,
Dad places one hand beneath my hands.
Like holding a milk jug from the fridge,
Except two jugs,
My heart beats faster,
Because he is right.

"Very heavy."

"This heavy gun kills people,

  These are not toys,

  And if it is okay with you,

I don't ever want to see you with plastic guns again.

I don't think it is very fun or funny.

It isn't your fault,

I know whose it is.

This gun will always be in here,

You don't ever need to go in here,

And I definitely never want you to pick up this gun or any gun.

  Do you know the only time you should ever pick up a gun?"

"Never."

"Wrong, but close,"

He reaches for the safe door,

"You only pick up a gun and shoot to protect your family,"

He closes the safe door.

LIVING WITH ALCOHOLISM

I believe that I cause bad nights anytime I eat purple grapes,

Because one night I ate purple grapes,

And it was a bad night.
My cousin asks me,
"Why are you jumping over the white carpet?"
Last time I didn't,
It was another bad night.

HOW TO CATCH A BOY'S ATTENTION

Falling in love with him,
He looks so different,
Bright red hair to his shoulders,
A river dribbling from his nostrils to his lips.
He sounds so different,
I follow him,
I chase him,
I poke him,

All day.
I sit with him and two girls,
I am jealous of those girls,
Before they even talk.
I don't know what they say,
I am not listening.
But he is listening,
So I start talking.
"My dad told me he is going to kill me tonight."

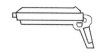

"WHAT?"
She screams in my ear.
"REALLY?"
The other girl cries out.
"Yeah, he is."
"Why?"
He asks me sadly.
"He just is, he didn't tell me why."
A bunch of questions,
Which I didn't expect.
They are all really upset,
Which I didn't expect.
One girl is mad,
Which I didn't expect.
She says I am lying.

I don't give in,
He is on my side.
"With his gun,"
I smile.

PART TWO: THE JOURNAL

INTRODUCTION TO
THIS TRANSITION

Dear past self,
It's time to start writing again.
Write every day,
A little bit,
When you can.
No pressure,
Just love.
Love, future self.

THE TRUTH PART II

I'm very, very, very tired.

THE FANTASY

He is a very beautiful man,
I don't know how old he is.
He loves me though,
Loves me very much.
He buys us an ivy-covered cottage,

Near Rocky Mountain National Park.
We are always alone there,
When we want to be.
He grows me daisies,
He decorates the floor with petals and sawdust.
I have pasta with extra olive oil
Every night with him.
We swim in the warm pond by the house,
Brushing against lily pads,
And spots of snow.
And when shit hits the fan,
I can always be with him,
He is always awaiting me,
And I am always awaiting him.

VOICES IN MY HEAD: #1 THE WHO I COULD HAVE BEEN IF ONLY

The girl who never changes,
A sweet Angel,
She has always known everything.
The all-knowing girl,
She has always been about heart,
Never material.
She always knows what matters most.
Her home is the world,

Always in childhood.
She is loved,
And Always will be.
My dear girl,
Who will always be beautiful.
Parts of herself she hates,
But everyone else loves.
She is now a sad girl,
Poisoned by a man.
I love her,
I want to see her natural,
Happy again.

VOICES IN MY HEAD: #2 FREE WILL, THE WOMAN

If my fingers had a more articulate talent,
I would try to sketch the exquisite,
The powerful image of the woman.
The evidently uncomfortable loveseat,
No challenge for her sculpted posture,
Able to turn any scene into a pedestal.
"Is it all right if I smoke in here?"
Her risen brows,
Manicured to symmetry.
"Sure, may I have one?
I won't tell my mother,
I don't tell her much anyways,

If I ever say anything at all."
My heart laughs,
What an awkward exposure of my life.
The woman takes the place of my heart,
Laughing loudly,
Her accent potent through her teeth.
She touches each cigarette,
Then hands me one with two fingers.
"You smoke,
Are you addicted?
When did you start?"
I feel like an important specimen,
Placed under a microscope,
Part of the most important hypothesis of the Earth.
"I don't,
I don't smoke,
But I'd like to start."
I let her light the end,
I inhale,
Hard and proud.
I feel an ashy wind blow a gust into my throat,
My nose coughs.
The woman smiles,
"That's why I started,"
Smoke dots out her nose,
And I wonder if it's on purpose.
"Because I could."
"What else do you do because you can?"
Eyeing her gold watch against her pearl wrist,
She looks at me with dark eyes in a dark way,
"Everything."

"So you can do everything?"
She exhales a thin line,
"Yes."
I bite the inside of my cheek,
"Can I do everything?"
She smiles,
"Although you and I just met,
I feel as though you are seeking a savior out of me.
What is it that you want to learn to do,
That you believe I can help you achieve?"
My jaw drops,
Smoke pouring over my lower lip.
I want to live in her short black sleekened tangles,
So I can just be a part of her mysterious divinity.
"My question involves men.
Why do they say that we need them,
When you and I can be like this,
With no man in the room?"
The woman rises,
Too quickly,
From the loveseat.
She walks to me,
Falls to her knees,
Pinches my chin,
I look into her eyes,
"Never fall to your knees in your life,
Except before a child."

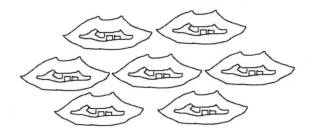

A PLACE THAT USED TO
BE A SWIMMING POOL

Wednesday after school,
We drive to the valley.
Catch a ride with whomever,
We are going to the same place.
Cops don't come here,
It is too far out.
Sitting in the shelter house,
You can see everything,
But you can't hide.
There will be a frisbee game,
Waiting on two more people.
Girls don't play,
We smoke,
We watch,

We talk.
Look up to the hills,
There's more people up there.
You can't see them,
But they can see you.
I go there to cry,
There's a bench to lay on,
My best friend put it there.
My heart has been hurting,
I really don't know why,
And I feel so lonely.
Some days,
I'm not sure what I'm looking for.
But in the valley,
No one asks what you are looking for.
Do you want to share?
Did you do something different with your hair?
Are you doing okay?
I don't know you well,
But we still care.
This territory belongs to the boys.
Some days,
I am the one who catcalls.
I only offer stories,
I never buy,
I never play.
My girls are with me,
We are older,
We are used to it,
We started young.
If these boys didn't keep half an eye out,

I would not have made it.
They teach me to be self-reliant,
But I can ride in the backseat.
My dad teaches me,
I'd rather die of cancer,
Then look up to a man.
The boys teach me,
I can do both.

VACATION

Pretty cloudy,
Very muggy,
Not many people,
Maybe a dozen here at the beach.
Most of them are in one way or another returning to the spot they came from.
They are kinda sorta thankful they came out to enjoy this morning,
Yet very eager to forget about it,
Ready to see what other fruits the low hanging trees of life have to offer them today.
But I see a boy shuffling a deck of cards.
An hour later,
He introduces himself to my parents,
Takes me to get ice cream.

I order a vanilla milkshake,
He thinks that is weird.
"What do you want to do now?"
I lie,
"I don't know."
The voices in my head,
"Why are you kissing?"
I'd rather die of cancer,
"You know, I'm not mad."
Then to ever consider the idea,
"I just want to know what's going on."
Of looking up to a man.

In the parking garage,
I whisper,
"You know I can't go that far."
As if he knows,
As if I know him at all.

VACATION
REFLECTIONS

What blows my mind,
Is that he wanted me,
And I wore no makeup.
I drink vanilla milkshakes for the whole summer.
Then I switch to peach.
Oh yeah,
Then there was that nice beach.

VOICES IN MY HEAD:
#3 MY DEATH WISH

We walk inside,
We feel like we own the place.
A plaid scarf around my head,
Smoking a lousy cigarette.
I don't like to smoke cigarettes,
They make my mouth so dry,
It hurts to smile.
"Hey guys,"
A man is sitting in a torn up recliner,
Two others sit close by,
Eyes on me.
They look like women,
They can recognize I am a woman,
But I do not appear as a woman.

A big round table between us and them.
Thin, small lines of white powder,
Strung rays off the hot sun.
"What is this?"
I don't know why I ask.
I don't know why I don't wait.
Dollar bill out of my pocket,
First line is mine,
I own the place.
And the rest are mine,
I own the world.

No one speaks,
Silent,
Maybe I'm not even here.
My friends,
Expressionless,
Dead.
Burnt out.
We are getting older.
The reclined man frowns,
"I don't know why you did that,
You are going to die now.
Well,
Not now,
But extremely soon."

GYM CLASS

I wear a Rogue Wave shirt,
Still has my old babysitter's smell.
My mom's too tight,
Too long shorts,
She says they are twenty years old.
I don't enjoy being on a team,
The good players are always close friends.
I am not the worst,
But it's clear who always gets picked first.
I hate running the most,
Then I hate the way they look at me.
Sometimes I bleed through my pants,
And sometimes I fake cramps.
My shoes are also my mom's,
At least I'm not the girl wearing Toms.
I know I'm not alone in the way I feel,
And I know to some this class means more.

I don't feel like I get anything out of this,
But I see the best getting stronger,
The best are getting better.
My favorite is the weight room,
Because I do my own thing.
I like that I can adjust weight,
I can wear my headphones.
I guess I don't feel I belong,
It could be different if friends were here.
These games just feel humiliating,
I hide in the bathroom,
Scratching wax out of my right ear.

Maybe it's all in my head,
But I am uncomfortable here.

THE FANTASY PART II

The sun makes it rain warm drops,
Upon the frozen Northern ground
That I step my feet upon.
I want to see the brightest,
Of the brightest part of the sun.
In a nice, long,
Driven venture towards the Southwest.
With my best friends,
Who bring my new friends,
I've waited a little while,
And I'll wait a little while longer.
It will be a beautiful life,
I will buy it for a good offer.
I'm sick of this frozen ground,
Stopping me from feeling the world.
I can't wait any longer,
To be warm and be part of that beauty.
It is waiting for us in a cottage by the sand.
We will go through it all hand and hand.

AFTER DAD LEAVES

Dad always told me my feet smell like stinky cheese.
My boyfriend's farts all smell like stinky cheese.

HIGH SCHOOL

She goes to school,
Just like years before.
She is sassy,
Men like her more.
I ask her kindly,
Will you be my friend?
Or would you rather me consider you dead?
She holds the cross,
It hugs her chest.
She says honey,
We are such a mess.
She breaks down the trees between our lives,
We play as two girls,
Home alone,
Drunken housewives.
I finish a school day,
I made a new friend.
She prays,
Like a child in strife.
I ask why pray,
You have it all,
Is there something more you want?

CHRISTMAS

Writing is my only outlet for this feeling I have.
I question what is important to me right now.
We may move away and
I may be left to decide what the best investment of
myself is.
When I think about this,
The solution seems simple.
I will stay here,
Where I know,
Because it's possible.
I know I will be sad either way,
But I don't want to wonder what if.
But If we go,
I must commit
To a new life.
It will need to be a must that I can trust.

AN APOLOGY TO MY NOW SINGLE MOM

I'm sorry,
For playing music while you watch the news,
For not doing the dishes until I feel like it,
That I broke the laundry lid with my laundry,
For cursing at you,
That I always lose my house key,
That I wake you up every morning,
That I wreck my car,
That I don't watch television with you,
That I go out most weekend nights,
That I wear your clothes instead of mine,
That I sing terribly at you,
For putting stupid pictures on the internet,
For yelling at you in public,
For stealing your makeup,
For texting when we are out to lunch,
For playing my CD's when you are driving,
For asking you for gas money,
For not talking to you.

THE TRUTH PART III

Again, I feel totally dissatisfied.
I've held out for a decent amount of time as of yet.
I'm beginning to feel not so good, though.
I'm comfortable admitting to myself that if I don't
find a better social environment,
I will never find a way to make it.
I don't want to go to places anymore.
I don't want to complain anymore.
I don't want to athletically train to look sexy.
I don't want to toe the line between taken and a
whore.
I don't want to play a game to win.
I don't want the sinful to preach to me about sin,
I want an interactive story that is not my own life.
If I don't have anyone to help,
Or anyone to fuck,
I'm unsure of where to turn.
A lot of this world can really suck.
Alone,
It is hard to concentrate,
And for myself I am starting to feel concern.

SITTING BEHIND
THE DRUGSTORE

"I just want to fucking learn something new,
No desk,
No chair,

Just those wheels."
"Wheels?"
"Yeah, wheels,
Those wheels!"
"You wanna learn to ride his skateboard?"
"I want to learn to ride my own fucking skate-board."
"All right,
Well why don't you?"

DEAD YOUTH IN A
DEAD TOWN

"I wish he had never died, my love."
"Baby, when your life gets hard,
You sure are quick to come back to him."
"It was the last time that everything felt okay
Without me trying to make everything right."

"Do you want some wine?"
"I want to disappear."
"I'd rather you skate."
"I'm going to shave my head."
"As long as you keep shaving everything else."
"Sometimes I really hate my life without you."
"You always hate your life."
"He would have never said that."
"Are you sure about that?"

LOSING MYSELF

"I think you're being hard on yourself."
"Are you kidding?
I hate everything except myself."
"I think you're in a lot of pain."
"And if I am?"
"Have you thought of working through any of that?"
"Have I thought of working through any of that?"
"Yes,
Have you thought of working through any of that?"
"Go fuck yourself."

THE PART THAT'S HARD
TO TALK ABOUT

"Dad?"
"Oh my little girl, how are you doing?"

MATH PARTNERS
AND PROBLEMS

"Do you believe in God?"
I am nervous,
What if he has changed?
How has he changed?
I don't lie,
"Yes."
"After he died,
She had a vision.
A giant mountain,
God standing above it,
Holding him up.
God seemed to be taking him away.
And then,
God held up a ribbon in the other hand.
And then,
The vision was clear,
God won,
Not cancer."

THE IDENTITY OF
A TEENAGER

I like playing board games by myself,
Yes I am embarrassed about it.
I want to publish things,
That make people feel things.
I want to give others good ideas.
But I've been busy,
Because not too long ago,
Someone called the cops on us,
A giant group of us.
We drove an hour to get away,
But we left our frisbees behind,
Our phone numbers on the inside.

if found,
return to
the valley

WARNINGS FROM MY TEACHER PART II

"You again."
Me again.
"This year, what is it with you?"
I have been late.
"All the time. What's your excuse today?"
I have excuses.
Traffic,
My friend was supposed to,
I was supposed to,
I was here but,
I choose truth.
I slept in.
He sighs,
So disappointed.
Me too, sir.

"You're slipping away."
I know, sir.
"You're surrounded by bad apples."
He's the apple of my eye though.
"You need to keep your eye on the prize."
My prize to me one day will be a surprise.
"Next time, it's going to be worse."
Some days I feel I was born to be a curse.
"Anywhere else, you would be a fly on the wall."

I want to fly away so I could really have it all.
"I expect better from you."
No one in these school halls has any clue.
"I need you to shape up your life."
A lot of us hurt ourselves but it's not always a knife."

"I don't want to see you in here again."
I'm a fly on the wall.
I've come to tell you your fortune.
"Promise me you'll do better?"
You will be promoted soon and will have to start sleeping in your den.
"What do you have to say for yourself?"
Nothing, dude.

REALIZING SOMETHING GREATER IS GOING ON HERE

It just hit me,
Just now,
I can't be the only person thinking about these things.
It must be a chronicle to feel so uncomfortable on this planet.
I should know,
I watch movies,
I talk to the people,
I read books,
I experience.
It is just so hard to believe that I am not alone,
When the feeling is presently tingling inside me.
It is like my soul is heavily present,
Telling me that this is the stress I am meant for.
Or maybe that is my Guardian Angel in my ear.

But myself,
I feel so differently than the wisdom that I know.
That is what makes it so difficult to respond,
At least in the ways I know I could.

GOODBYE TO ALL
MY FRIENDS

.

I have slept with a lot of people,
There have been many slow nights.
My heart has broken,
And I have made a lot of people cry.
There are many things I wish did not happen,
A lot of cleaning up to do.
Our parents regret giving us the basement,
They regret being out of town so much.
My family has broken apart,
My school has built a bigger one.
We have all done awful things,
And always had each other's backs.
Sleeping in strange places,
Waking up in stranger ones.
I have said horrible things,
Felt some unspeakable things.
I have violated privacy and spaces,
I have given some good things bad meanings.

But things are now changing,
These things no longer matter.
Because people are leaving,
There is a new plan,
Giving this town a new flavor.
It hurts much stronger,
Once again the family is changing,
Missing friends,
Missing faces.
Why does everyone have to go?
And to such beautiful places.
Another year I am left alone,
It's harder to rebuild on my own.
Help me find my way to my new home.
I have a lot of fear facing a new year.
But I digress,
Because today is your day.
We are at your mom's house,
And we are having a party.
Your life will change there,
My life will change here.
I am so frustrated,
You are so happy.
The things you will do,
The freedom you've earned.

It's hard to say goodbye,
But for our peace of mind,
My heart will try to learn.

VOICES IN MY HEAD: #4 THE IMAGINARY PEN PAL

Hello, my companion.
This morning,
I heard a man say something,
Resonating with my stance in this world.
He said,
"Negativity almost had me defeated,
But here I am back on my feet."
And so I thought of you.
I don't have much time,
My intention is to inform you,
I have you in my mind.
I know you are enjoying this feeling,
Holding this piece of paper in your hand.
I've got sickness inside me,
But there is also medicine.

PART THREE: POCKET NOTEBOOK

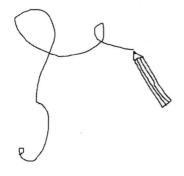

DEAR GOD

What do I feel?
My sense of light,
Art with surgency,
I am worshipping,
With urgency.
I am energy.
My heart, God,
Sends signals to my brain,
It feels like pressure.
My heart, God,
Builds on that pressure.
My heart, God,
Is a light antenna,
Technology meeting peace,
Spirituality meeting our information.
My heart, God,
Is in the midst of transformation.
I am a snake, God,
Shedding layers of communication.
What act of kindness today,
To lead me to mourn my former selves.
I am strong,
I am brave,
I am responsible,
I am accountable.
God, I am paying attention.

MOVING TO A NEW PLACE

Do I belong here?
How do I fit in?
Do I fit in?
What am I doing here?
Why am I here?
What am I pretending to be?

DATING

My boyfriend always thinks i am pregnant.
His biggest fear is that he will be connected to me
long Term without his consent.
Me violating time and space.
It would be a terminal illness.
I am never pregnant.
I am always his fear.
I am always a cow,
A time bomb,
A carrier of the virus,
Of long-term connection.

WHAT IS NEUROSIS?

She tells me I am neurotic,
Too neurotic,
To not receive full truth
From the man I love.
Scratching my head,
She doesn't know me well,
Not well enough to know who I am.
A Natural Born Liar,
In mental rehabilitation.
I know I am restless,
My ego is demanding,
I know what I don't want.
For someone I love
To open up the crown of my head,
Only for neurosis to spew out.
Now that I'm aware,
I have been trying to hide it.
But I know he knows.
So I have a new idea,
I'm going to start making my own decisions again,
I think that could help the neurosis disappear.
You know,
One time I did think I was pregnant,
And I told no one.

FIRST DAY OF WORK

My favorite outfit to wear to the office is a black and white long-sleeved business polo.

THE BLOOD OF
OUR PARENTS

I wake up to,

"Excuse me,"
A policewoman,
Tapping my shoulder,
With her pistol.
I shoot up.
"Yes, ma'am,"
Gaining focus,
She is a security guard,
I am in a waiting room.
"Who are you here for?"
Checking my surroundings,
The waiting room is empty,
Except for me,
The guard,
And her pistol.
It is pitch black outside,
I hear the Food Network.
I remember hearing that,
Earlier.
I must have been awake,
Earlier.
Maybe within a couple hours,
Because it was the same show.
It's in the middle of the night.
"My dad."

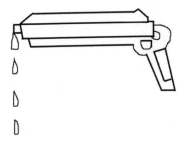

How could this guard not know?
I am the only person here.
Maybe she is new on shift.
Although something about her,
Was very familiar.

TALKING YOURSELF
OUT OF IT

I just want to start a new life,
I want a blank page.
But what if I just slightly change the words,
Just start living,
Just start moving.
You can fix it later,
Revamp your whole damn soul.
One hundred years is a life that may not be good,
But death is death.

DEAD YOUTH IN A
DEAD TOWN PART II

An old classmate of mine messages me,
I ask her if she has any advice for me,
To which she replies,
"Even one breath is significant,
Don't be hard on yourself."

This classmate,
She is responsible for me meeting someone,
A very important friend to me,
May he rest in peace.

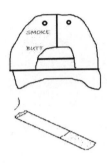

ROOMMATES

"I had a wild dream last night,"
He laughs,
Sitting down to join breakfast.
I say
"Wait for her to sit down too,
Before you do tell,"
Not looking up from my book.
"Good point,
I will wait,"
He smiles,
Grabs a blueberry bagel.

"Is this really necessary?"
She sits down,
"Is what really necessary?
I ask calmly.
She has had this unusual,
Very impatient mood.
"I am just not interested in hearing dreams."
I look up from my book,
Peering at her,
"People do not speak to just catch your interest."
Speaking my truth gives me a rush nowadays,
"If there is something more important
That you feel the need to share with us,
Please do.
But don't cut others down."
I turn back to my book.

"You were in my dream,"
He says to her,
Taking a bite of his bagel.
She stares at her plate.
Something is wrong with her,
I intend to find out what it is.

THOUGHTS AT MY NEW FAVORITE CAFE

She pours me a mimosa,
I am thinking about this man.
It is Saturday morning,
Almost my lunch time.
He isn't the only person I am thinking about.
I am thinking about all of them.
God, I swear
You blessed me with the best people of the world.
They're all somewhere in my life,
And I have the worst relationship skills
So bad,
It is hard to believe.
I don't mean to be abusive.
I don't know how to communicate my love for
these individuals,

They impact my life,
An astronomical amount.
Right now,
I am sulking because of myself,
I am sitting in this very nice place.
I lie about the mimosa,
I have not ordered.
I cannot tell if I am growing,
Or shrinking into my own despair.
Or maybe this is the place I change today.

Could I write a song,
Could I write a poem?
Could I write both?
When I just put my fingers to it,
I am suddenly creating,
I can edit later.
There's this photo on the bathroom wall,
Makes me vocalize as I take a pee,

"Just start writing,
You can edit later,
Rewrite the whole damn thing.
One hundred pages is a book that may not be good,
But blank pages are blank pages."

THE BACHELORETTE
AUDITION TAPE

I put my tongue in my sideways grown wisdom
tooth,
Scooping black pepper out.
I have been cooking the same healthy breakfast
these past three mornings.
Two cage-free eggs,
Kale,
Mushrooms,
Avocado,
Kiwi.
Then the coffee,
2% milk.
The food is covered in cumin,
My favorite.
Then the black pepper,
Then salt.
I found out some news,
I have low blood pressure.
I try to remember to not keep myself away from
sodium,

Although I heard sodium is bad, too.
My point is,
This whole life thing,
I'm trying.
And there is evidence for that.

VIOLENCE PART III

I step up to the podium,
I look no one in the eye.
They will hear me,
Tap tap.
"There were many good things about my father.
He did not sleep.
I have heard of some known scholars to be the same.
It is a unique super power,
I could always count on him to be awake.
This was helpful when I had bad dreams.
My father was also an artist.
In the kitchen,
With computers,
With radios,
With instruments,
With languages.
He raised me to be the same."
Deep breath.
"My dad told me stories about the old days,
He told everyone stories about the old days.
He was the one always calling them old days.
I know that some of the old days,

They weren't even his old days.
He was able to retrieve memories from past lives of others,
But never his own.
In my opinion,
It was a poor glitch in his life's pattern,
Ended up being part of his downfall in addiction,
And his own end in violence.
I believe that if my father could have remembered his past life,
Maybe he could have retrieved old tricks,
Maybe they could have saved his conscience.
Kind of like when you accidentally delete that important document on your computer.
You can only maybe retrieve it with the help of Others,
Or by previously investing time into backing it up
On another device.
My dad was never good at backing up tricks and Memories with other people,
No good at relationships.
And quite frankly I don't think I am either."
Look up,
Back down,
"I had to make a choice a few years ago,
A choice that would ultimately change the course of my life,
With no possibility of going back.
I could argue that I make these choices daily,
But I must emphasize that this was an ultimate change.

I felt I had to decide between higher education,
And the quality of life for my father.
My father,
Who began to see his pistol differently.
There are many stories that led up to this decision,
That I don't want to talk about.
The way I thought back then,
I felt certain that my father was not choosing his own life.
And I was certain that someone had to.

My mom tried,
But her strong will had to protect her own life,
And my life.
I chose my higher education,

I cut my father from my life.
I do love talking about him.
In another life
He may have chosen me,
Chosen my sisters,
Chosen family.
Maybe in a life
Where he can sleep on things more."
Deep breath.
"I could argue,
I could say that it's my fault that dad is not here
today,
But these days,
I love myself too much for that version of truth.
See,
The good thing about a young child who learns to
lie well,
Is the possibility of using that lesson in the future.
To not dwell on dark truths.
The decision I made
Led me to sitting in a library,
Studying the urban geography of a city in Ohio,
A city I had never been to.
I was learning that at the time,
This was a city with the most people,
Leaving the city,
Moving to the suburbs.
This may not sound important,
I assure you it never was important to me.
But this is where my brain was when I met that very
Important friend.

May these two men rest in peace."

A YEAR INTO MY
NEW CAREER

To be a young woman,
A little fish in a little city,
There are things I consider,
There are things I know.
I will always choose love,
Over the American dream.
At the same time,
I now know I will always do my best
To make the most logical decision
That is available to me at that moment.
I am not in love.
I have a great job.
There is a fly on the wall,
It has come to tell me my fortune.
One part of my life will turn upside down,
Very, very soon.

The fly and I don't know much more,
But he says it will be drastic.
I consider that I am ready for it,
I consider that I am ready for anything.
I consider that I will let it rock and roll.
I will always choose love,
Above all else that is possible.
Goodnight, God.

THE LITTLE THINGS
IN A BIG LIFE

I wear a short skirt and sports bra.
If you don't like it, we'll fight outside the bar.
He says,
"You all right baby,
Come sit on my face."
And I just want city police to stop using mace.
Muchas cosas,
Your behavior just shows us.
My lips are chapped and my man just crapped,
I'm feeling so tired,
Feeling confused,
And I know it's sad I know she's being abused.
En mi camino, pero estoy solita.
I'm gonna travel in the city, eh.
I'm gonna live in the city, eh.
Mi y my itty bitty titty,
I've lived with people that make me feel shitty.

Yo vivo sola,
Yo perreo sola,
Yo hablo sola,
Me encanta la ciudad,
And I really miss my dad.

VOICES IN MY HEAD: #2 FREE WILL, THE WOMAN PART II

The woman drops to her bottom,
Lays down.
"Take that cigarette out of your mouth."
My reflex,
Immediate obedience,
Yet my cigarette is not finished,
I do not understand.
"Why did you do as I say?"
I look at my cigarette,
Strings of smoke,
Fishtailing off the faded red,
But I look at it in a different way,
In a questioning way,
"I'm not sure."
"Maybe because you trust me?"

"Maybe,
I don't know,
I don't normally do what people ask me to do."
"I know."
She stands up,
Walks to the coat rack,
Takes my father's baret,
Places it on her head,
Turns to me,
A strange look on her face.
She looks desperate,
She looks weak.
She walks toward me,
Like she can't wait to be closer to me.
I put the cigarette back in my mouth,
I watch.
Parts of my body feel limp,
Others feel warm,
She sits next to me.
She sits too close.
Her lips to my ear,
"Will you take that cigarette out of your mouth?"
I suddenly get it,
I chuckle,
"No, ma'am,
I can do anything,
I can do everything I want."
She lays back on the floor,
Puts her cigarette out on my rug.
I smile,
Put my cigarette out in my ashtray,

"This relationship is going to work out great,"
I grab my water,
"I may rather die of cancer,
But that doesn't mean I have to."
She disappears.

A MORNING IN NEW YORK CITY

One last thing about waking up early,
After declaring a life change for myself.
Power on Earth comes from lifeforce,
Definitely not money.
The will to stay alive starves all else.
Laying in this big bed during the day,
Staring up at building terraces.
There is a pot of flowers on the railing,
Strongly resembling a blond woman in a colorful t-
Shirt,
She is staring down at me, too.
This moment deeply resembles older mornings,
In my parents' bedroom.
There is a sudden pressure in my stomach.
I stand up,
In front of the window,
Now staring at the apartment archway next door.
The light fixture,
It looks like a blond woman in a blue shirt,
She is staring right at me.

There is a part of me,
I believe this woman follows me.

She whispers,
"It's okay."
"So I've been kind of kicking myself,
I am having internal intimidation of my goals.
I do not think I will drink today either,
Or at least just not tomorrow.
I don't know if it is still true,
That I have the world at my fingertips.
I'm not certain,
If I can do whatever I want.
I'm not certain,
If I can do whatever well."

She whispers,
"It's okay."

ABOUT THE AUTHOR

Kelly Fernandez

 This is Kelly's first published content, a taste of her thoughts and images that she wants to put to bed before moving forward. Her creative background stems from short story writing, yet she has recently been inspired by various poets that push her to experiment with more vulnerable writing. Before completing this book, Kelly has been experimenting with collaborating different rules and formatting of writing to tell a story that can put the reader in the scene. This is her first time openly sharing her writing since middle school and she aims to inspire others to start sharing again. Kelly studied social work and found passion for the world of public health. You can find her dancing in her kitchen or asking a cafe if she connect her bluetooth to their speaker.

Made in the USA
Middletown, DE
07 September 2020